Don't be a bully, Billy

A Cautionary Tale

Phil Roxbee Cox

Illustrated by Jan McCafferty

Edited by Jenny Tyler
Designed by Non Figg

Meet Billy.

Billy is a bully.

...and everyone begs,

"Don't be a bully, Billy!"

But Billy keeps on bullying.

Billy the bully kicked Kevin...

6

...and kicked Kevin cried,

"Don't be a bully, Billy!"

and rubbed his knee.

Billy the bully shook Shaun...

...and shaken Shaun shouted,

"Don't be a b-b-bully, Billy!"

and tried to stop sh-sh-shaking.

Billy the bully picked on Paula...

...and picked-on Paula pleaded,

"Don't be a bully, Billy!"

and wiped away her tears.

Billy the bully chased Charlie...

...and chased Charlie panted,

"Don't be a bully, Billy!"

and hid around the corner.

It's Monday morning.
Billy the bully is
threatening Theo.

Then, on the way to class,
he barges into Belinda...

At lunchtime, Billy the bully pushes Peter into his pudding...

16

Billy snatches Bob's ball, and Bob says,

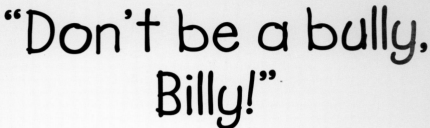

"Don't be a bully, Billy!"

"Give it back, it's mine!"

"Make me!"
says Billy the bully.

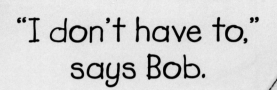

"I don't have to," says Bob.

"Meet my **Big Brother.**" Bob points up to the sky.

21

"Hi!" says Bob's big brother.
"You're coming for a ride!"

"HELLLLP!"
hollers helpless Billy...

23

But Billy's bullied
schoolmates simply shout,
"Bye-bye, Billy!"

and happily head for home.